# Before the Mermaid's Tale

## A Stunning Villain Back Story

Michelle Deerwester-Dalrymple

THE BEFORE... SERIES

Copyright 2023 Michelle Deerwester-Dalrymple  All rights reserved

Cover Art: licensed by Canva.com

Interior Formatting: Atticus

All rights reserved. In accordance with the U.S. Copyright Act of 1976, the scanning, uploading, distribution, or electronic sharing of any part of this book without the permission of the author constitutes unlawful piracy of the author's intellectual property. If you would like to use the material from this book, other than for review purposes, prior authorization from the author must be obtained. Copies of this text can be made for personal use only. No mass distribution of copies of this text is permitted.

This book is a work of fiction. Names, dates, places, and events are products of the author's imagination or used factiously. Any similarity or resemblance to any person living or dead, place, or event is purely coincidental.

**Don't forget to grab** your bonus *To Dance in the Glen* **ebook about Gavin** and learn what happened before he and Jenny met! Click the image below to receive *The Heartbreak of the Glen*, the free Glen Highland Romance short ebook, in your inbox, plus more freebies and goodies!

Click here:

https://view.flodesk.com/pages/5f74c62a924e5bf828c9e0f3

# Contents

1. Chapter One — 1
2. Chapter Two — 11
3. Chapter Three — 17
4. Chapter Four — 24
5. Chapter Five — 31
6. Chapter Six — 45
7. Chapter Seven — 56
8. Chapter Eight — 61

Read More! — 69

Excerpt from Before the Glass Slipper — 70

Excerpt from Before the Cursed Beast — 73

About the Author — 77

Also By Michelle — 78

## Chapter One

*WHAT DOES SHE WANT now?*

That was always the eternal question when Atheana called for me.

My royal purple and blue iridescent mermaid tail was a stunning combination of cool, oceanic hues that reflected the wavy sunlight as I swam too close to the surface. My scales shimmered in a deep, indigo blue-black at my waist and gradually faded into a vibrant, rich purple towards my long, furling flukes. I loved flapping my fins so my scales sparkled in a prismatic glow.

With my tail undulating behind me, creating a mesmerizing pattern of blues and purples, and my silvery hair trailing like a bridal veil off my head, I raced toward Eldoris where my brother King Neptune awaited. His wife, Atheana, was pregnant with their fifth (*fifth!*) child, and Neptune had requested his sister, the revered sorceress, Nerissa – *me* – keep Atheana company. Six daughters, even with the royal mermaid and fish servants, were enough to try the most patient of people, and none were more patient than Atheana.

Even if it did make Neptune even more pretentious than he already was as my older brother and sea king. His attitude and condescending nature drove me to the brink sometimes.

More than sometimes. Often as of late.

As if I had nothing better to do.

Ginevra, Neptune's eldest, swam past in a flash of pinkish orange, her dark, drift-wood brown hair trailing behind her. I smiled at the mermaid and her sisters, who followed in their game, and my heart clenched in my chest. As Neptune's younger sister, I should have been married and having my own merchildren already, but Atheana's health and the duties of Eldoris had called, pushing my romance with bold and outlandish merman Nerio to the side again and again.

Was I jealous? Yes. Because it was my time for love and family, and here I was playing nursemaid to the queen once more.

His kingdom of Eldoris thrived because of my magic.

As the king's sister, I performed a large role in Neptune's kingship – how many times had my sea magic created waves or lightning storms that beat back the prying, spear-wielding humans from the surface?

My adoration for my sea-nieces was replaced by a knife of hate that drove a sour taste up my throat to my mouth. Was there anything worse in this world than a human?

Yes, a human bearing a harpoon.

For a moment, I wondered if there might be another reason Neptune asked me to stay near Atheana. Had the land-walkers come too close to the palace? Try to invade the royal sea-parks, coves, grottoes, and reefs?

Probably. Though Eldoris proper was far beneath the surface on the seafloor, many parts of the kingdom rose closer to the surface. Much closer.

Close enough for sailors and pirates and the algae-sucking worst of them all, *fishermen*, to peer into their private world and harm any fish that swam too close.

Land-walkers. The thought of them made the sour taste in my throat thicken until it choked me.

When I arrived at the barnacle and seaweed-covered castle, Atheana wasn't in her chambers, so I left through the rear archway to the palace sea garden. It was Atheana's favorite spot to have time away from her children, surrounded by a red coral reef wall and filled with creamy yellow sponges, purple sea anemones, bright green grassy seaweed, and a water-smoothed stone bench. Atheana sat upon that bench, her wide belly fit to burst under her turquoise green scales.

"Nerissa! What a pleasure to find you in my hali-garden. What brings you here?" She patted the side of the bench, and I swirled my deep purple-blue tail around myself to sit next to my brother's wife.

This pregnancy was taking a toll on the queen of the sea. Her skin, usually the color of the palest beach sand, was more the pallor of a fish's underbelly, sallow and sickly. Even her normally vibrant red-blonde hair seemed dim. But her smile made her entire face brighten through her algae-green-blue eyes, and I did not resist the urge to smile back.

"Neptune thought you might enjoy some company away from the children. I just saw them swim away." My voice trailed off as I pointed in the direction the mermaids had gone. Atheana gave an affectionate glance over her shoulder, then turned back to me. She rested her slender hand on my pointy, long-fingered one.

"I'm glad you're here. I have a favor to ask of you. Well, more of a secondary favor."

One silver eyebrow rose on my forehead. "A secondary favor?"

Atheana giggled out a trail of tiny bubbles. "You know how Neptune's birthday is coming up?"

I nodded. "I'll be at the birthday feast tonight."

"Yes, but his birthday is in two days, and I have asked Nerio to find a special gift for me."

The mention of Nerio made my heart flutter under my sea shells. My love. My heart. My everything. I had waited so long to marry him; even hearing his name brought twittering excitement. Taking a long breath of water, I focused back on Atheana.

"What's he getting?"

Atheana's smile faltered, and she leaned into me until only a few inches of water flowed between us. "A chalice. A *human* chalice."

I slapped my hand over my mouth. "Atheana! Why would you want to do such a thing? Does Neptune want a human chalice?"

Atheana giggled knowingly. "Yes. He found one deep in the sea a few weeks ago. It was gem-encrusted with barnacles. It must have been caught on the current from the shore or a sunken ship. He commented that it was too bad it didn't have a match, for he would have liked to toast us and our merpeople's health with a pair of human chalices."

An explosion of bubbling laughter burst out of me. Of course, Neptune would want to shake a fist at the humans, and using their own utensils to celebrate merpeople was just the way to do that.

"So, what's the secondary favor you need from me?" I asked.

"I think it will be difficult to find the match. Can you, well, do, something about that?"

I smirked. *Do something.*

Atheana might not like to say the word, but I knew what she meant.

*Magic.*

I wasn't a renowned sea-witch for nothing.

"You want a small spell to make sure he can find the chalice? You want me to find it for him?"

Atheana nodded, her smile widening. It seemed almost too big for her face.

"Yes! If you can tell Nerio where to find it, that would be wonderful. I'd really like to have it for Neptune's birthday."

I also nodded, mimicking her movement. "I'll help Nerio tomorrow."

Atheana reached her arms around my shoulder and hugged me. "Thank you, Nerissa. You are the best."

That night, as rippling sunlight dimmed beneath the depths and was replaced by dark waters, sleek fish and merpeople made their way through Eldoris to the palace for King Neptune's birthday feast.

Atheana earlier had whispered to me that he wanted to keep his actual birthday a private affair between just the two of them. A moue of resentment tightened my lips – I was Neptune's sister, after all. Shouldn't *I* be a part of any birthday celebration? Then I tossed my silver hair over my shoulder and tried to brush the thought away. Neptune was king, and if he wanted a private birthday with only Atheana and his children, that would happen.

Before I reached the arched entry to the palace's main hall, someone swam against me, pinning me under the seaweed awning. I breathed out bubbles of excitement.

*Nerio.*

I hadn't seen him in a couple of days, and my expectations of seeing him tonight had me strung tight. Now here he was, his cool arms around my waist and his face right in front of mine.

"You're a sight for sore eyes, Urs. Never let me agree to a scouting assignment from your brother again."

His blondish hair floated around his head as his dark green eyes, darker than his fins, sparkled at me. His eyes were like my own private grotto, and I could lose myself in them.

"I worried about you," I told him as a sly smile curled my full lips.

Nerio huffed out a bubbly laugh. "Not too much. I know you were watching me in your cauldron."

My smile rose higher on my right cheek. I had used the shimmery reflection of my cauldron to see where he was – it was one of my more effortless magic touches. My pot showed me what was going on anywhere in the sea, and I used it whenever I wanted to know what was going on under the surface.

Nerio knew me too well. But then, of course, he would. He and I had been friends for as long as I could remember. We had grown up swimming together in the vibrant coral reefs, exploring the hidden undersea caves, and playing hide and seek in kelp forests. Nerio had been Neptune's friend and became mine as we grew from tiny merchildren.

For a moment, we gazed at each other, our hearts beating as one. Then Nerio spoke, his voice barely above a whisper in the dark water.

"I love you," he said.

My smile slipped, and my heart throbbed achingly. "And I love you, Nerio."

He flapped his tail to surge closer to me until his face was shell's width from mine. "Marry me, then," he said in his raspy voice, making me quiver to the tips of my tail.

My heart froze in my chest. "Nerio –"

"No more excuses. No more 'Wait for Atheana's baby.' No more 'Wait until my brother approves.' I'm done waiting for you. Marry me. Tonight, tomorrow, the next day, now. I don't care. I just want you for my wife."

His hand had grasped mine and threaded our fingers together.

"Please, Nerissa. No more waiting." His begging voice was rich and vibrated with emotion.

I couldn't deny him. "Yes. Yes, a million times, yes, Nerio. As soon as my brother's birthday is over, we will wed."

Then he kissed me, his lips sleek and cool, until the giggle of several mermaids at the palace entrance interrupted us.

"Come on," Nerio said, tugging on my hand. "Let's join your brother for his feast."

As we swam through the gentle currents to the front of the palace, my joy was certain, complete. I knew, the same as I would if I had seen it in my cauldron, that our love would be strong enough to withstand anything that the ocean could throw at us.

I grinned widely as we joined the mermen and mermaid in the lustrous main hall.

I was sure of it.

That night, Neptune glowed as he sat beside Atheana, flanked by his daughters. His smile, partially hidden by his full graying blond beard, never left his face. Atheana, pale and wan as she was, wore her own smile as she looked up at the king of the sea.

Fishes swan by with plates and bowls, everything from kelp stew to seagrass, and pitchers of sparkling water from the underground sparkling pools. A myriad of colorful seaweed, bioluminescence fish, and glowing algae was placed around the room, adding brilliant light to the palace hall.

Honestly, it was a celebration to rival his past birthdays.

With a slight glance at his wife, Neptune stood from his seashell chair and spread his muscled arms wide.

"Thank you all for coming this evening! Another course of seasons under the sea, and I am grateful to my wife and daughters for celebrating it with me!"

*Wife and daughters.* My sneer twisted my face – I couldn't stop it – and Nerio shifted so his arm was in front of us as he turned to me.

"Have patience with him, Urs. You know he has always been this way since he wed Atheana. Do you think I would be any different with you? I don't see anyone else when you're in the room. Don't take the slight personally."

I sighed and placed my hand on Nerio's cool cheek. My sneer faded.

"You always know the right thing to say. You'll be the best husband, this I know."

Nerio grinned in a way that I knew meant a tease was coming.

"I'd stand up and announce my intention to marry you right now if I didn't think Neptune would lower his trident at me and filet me where I stood."

I slapped my hand over my mouth to hold back my barking laugh. Neptune would never forgive that interruption at his celebration. Nerio's smile widened, and he removed my fingers from my mouth and curled his hand around mine.

"Let's eat, drink, and celebrate. In three days, we'll announce our wedding and become the center of attention. And no one will be as happy as we are. Not even Neptune."

He kissed my hand and swiveled in his seat to return his focus to the sea king. I couldn't stop staring at his strong profile.

*Such an amazing merman, and he's all mine.*

## Chapter Two

THE NEXT DAY, I told Nerio where to find the chalice. From my mirrored cauldron, I couldn't quite see if the cup glinting in the sand was the exact same, but it was so very close that it might be from a similar set, if not the match. I hoped it would suffice.

It should. Atheana was asking for a lot once I saw where the chalice lay. Too close to the surface for my comfort, and I told Nerio that.

Nerio had kissed my nose before he left and told me not to worry. Being that close to the shore came with a measure of danger, but Nerio welcomed such a challenge.

"Close to the surface for us, but not close to shore for land–walkers," he had said.

He might be right – it wasn't like land-walkers swam to those indigo depths, and boats only covered a small part of the surface. Nerio's confidence in his ability to avoid any ships emanated from him in warm waves like an underwater volcano.

While he might not be worried about any land-walkers and their boats, I was.

Before he swam away, he leaned into my floating hair and placed his lips to my ear.

"As soon as I return, we will announce our marriage," he vowed. Then with a cool kiss upon my cheek, his red-gold fins flapped hard enough for my hair to swirl around my head in his wake.

As soon as he left, I headed to my private cave.

Neptune knew about it – I could not hide my long absences from the palace, so I had to tell him. But he was the only person aware of the dark recess holding my magical implements. He didn't mind because it kept my magic from the palace. Though he had his own power through his trident, it wasn't his, and it was contained in the weapon. No cauldrons or potions for that man. No magic with a wave of his fingertips. I don't know if he feared my power was greater than his, or if he didn't like to be reminded that my power was contained in my body and not a trident anyone might wield.

Either way, it was of no account. The private cave was my own, and I rushed toward the shadowy rocks to watch Nerio retrieve the chalice.

I had watched him before, when possible – keeping an eye on him, just for safety's sake. Not that I might be able to do much if he ran into trouble, but seeing him complete a mission and return heartened me.

Dark green seaweed and polyps dangled from the entry, which was surrounded by the skeleton of some ancient sea creature and large corals that hid most of the cave. I brushed the bulbous plants aside as I entered my private chambers.

I had tucked pink algae in the corners for a bit of color and set up a small vanity and mirror to the side in case I ever needed to rush from my cavern to the palace. Right now, though, my attention was on my cauldron – a multi-legged vessel that smoked with undersea gasses and formed a giant, mirror-like bubble when I used it for viewing.

Which I was doing now. With an upward flap for my hand, the gaseous smoke shifted, and a large bubble rose from the black pot. I raced to the cauldron and rested my palms on the edge as I leaned in to watch.

Nerio swam confidently toward the water's surface, his hunter-green eyes fixed on the glimmering object he had spotted from below. I admired his form as his body undulated under the waves. He was a proud and powerful creature, and I sensed that he believed nothing could harm him as he searched for the chalice in the shallows.

I bit my lip as I watched him approach the object. He lifted it, and I squinted to see the glint of encrusted gems shining in the sunlight. This close to the surface, the sun's rays were fine lines in the water, and the waves reflected on the sand. Without hesitation, he reached out to grab it, and a surge of excitement burst through me as his fingers closed around the treasure.

He had it! Now to get out of there and return to the deeper waters of the sea.

Then something broke through those watery sun rays. Nerio cried out, whipping his wide-eyed face toward the surface. My chest was hollow and aching as I swept my hands over the bubble to change the angle of my view and show what was on the surface.

*A boat! Land-walker fishermen!*

Nerio's mouth opened in surprise and pain. I watched with growing horror as another spear pierced through the water. He pulled his hand back, staring at the barbed hook lodged in his shoulder. The land-walkers were *fishing* for him!

"No!" I screamed as I raced out of my grotto, swimming to the shallows where Nerio was under attack.

If I didn't get to him in time, he'd be strung up on some fisherman's hook on his boat, and I would lose the love of my life forever.

Neptune's adviser, the young crab Tiberian, swam with three swordfish guards as I raced by.

"Tell Neptune to follow me! Now!" I shouted, flapping my tail harder, swimming as fast as my fluke could move.

One swordfish chased after me, and the waters churned as the others raced for the castle.

*It's not too late... it's not too late...* I kept chanting in my head as I careened through the water toward the shallows.

The light separated from the depths, shimmering light piercing the waves as the barbed spear had pierced Nerio. I didn't see him anywhere. Had the fisherman got him?

A cluster of bubbles emerged from a collection of coral and sea anemones. With a hesitant flap of my tail, I curved around the rock to find my nightmares had come true.

The land-walkers hadn't gotten him – at least there was that. But what they left behind . . .

Blood blended into the water, curling pinkish in the waves beating back against the seafloor. His blond hair moved with each shift of the water, and one of his hands extended as if reaching for me, begging me to help him.

Hot tears burned in my eyes. There was no helping him. It was too late.

My Nerio, my love, was gone. Only the shell of the merman remained. My watery breath caught in my gills as I gasped and tried to temper myself, but I was spinning out of control.

My tears mixed with the salty seawater as I moved to him. I wanted to scream, cry, pound my fists against the waves, yet my anger had to wait until I got Nerio home.

The swordfish swam under his other arm as I grabbed Nerio's hand. We'd carry him back to the palace together.

As we moved him, something gold clunked into the sand with a puff.

*The chalice.*

The cursed chalice. The gift Atheana wanted. The birthday gift for Neptune.

If she hadn't asked Nerio to find the match, this would never have happened.

My heart hardened in my chest as we swam to Eldoris. As I carried the body of the man I loved, I vowed I'd never forgive either of them for this.

Atheana and Neptune were responsible. Even if they didn't know it yet, they had robbed me of the purest love ever known to the sea. And as such, they would know the sheer volume of my pain, an ache that drove deeper than the darkest depths of the ocean.

Before we left, I snatched the chalice up with the curled fluke of my tail.

I'd make sure Neptune got his cursed birthday gift.

## Chapter Three

Neptune met me as we neared the palace, his face a bearded mask of dread. Every line on his face stood out on his skin, and his eyes searched my face before shifting to Nerio's limp body. With a flap of his tail, he moved forward to take Nerio from me.

"No!" I shouted, moving to block him. "I've got him!"

"Please, Nerissa," he said in a voice laden with sorrow. "He was like a brother to me, my oldest friend. My pain is real. Let me do this."

I didn't move, but the swordfish guard gave up his place so his king could carry Nerio's body.

We brought him to the main hall of the palace, where he would lay for two days while the merpeople paid homage and their respects to the great man. Then the swordfish guard would carry his body to the underwater volcano and place his body inside the smoky mouth.

I didn't leave his side the entire time. Atheana waddled into the main hall, presumably to offer me a shoulder to cry on, but I had no tears left. I had shed them all as we brought Nerio home. I wouldn't have given her the pleasure even if I had tears left to shed. Now all I had was anger tinged with sorrow. She stopped halfway in the hall when she noted my incensed stare, then turned her attention to Nerio.

In her hand, she carried a large shell to place on his chest and bury him with to take to the afterwater. She rested her hand on his chest, and that was the final draw for me. I lost all reasoning.

"Don't touch him!" I screamed as I flipped my fins hard to rush her, blocking her from approaching him. "You're the reason he's dead, so don't you touch him!"

Atheana froze, and turned her shocked aquamarine eyes to me. Neptune had entered the hall and heard me and raised his stern blue gaze to the scene.

"Nerissa, I know you think –"

"I don't think," I hissed at Atheana, poking my finger into her chest, "I know. This never would have happened if you hadn't been looking for that chalice, the birthday gift. The cursed birthday gift."

I rushed to the other side of the stone table holding the body of my love and grabbed the infernal, gem-encrusted cup and threw it at her. She managed to get her hands up before the cup smacked her face, and it floated to the floor.

That cursed chalice.

"Nerissa! What are you doing? How dare you throw something at Atheana!"

I spun on my brother, my fury reaching a fevered pitch. "Oh, Poseidon, help her, that she might get bonked on the head by a cup. Nerio is dead, Neptune! Dead! And you're worried about a cup!"

The tears returned, squeezing from my eyes as I shouted and rushed and flailed. I was out of control. I had no control! I had nothing – *nothing!* – now that Nerio was dead. And he was worried about a thrown chalice?

"It's her fault!" I shrieked like a siren as if screaming loud enough would bring Nerio back to my rocky shores. "Her fault and yours! He was killed over a stupid cup! Almost caught by fishermen land-walkers, all because of your stupid gift!"

"Enough!" Neptune shouted, and the fishes and crustaceans in the hall skittered to the edges or found the nearest door. No one wanted to face Neptune when anger took hold.

But I didn't care. If he was hurting over Nerio's death, then I was dying. How could he begin to compare his pain to mine? And then chastise me over the cup on top of it all?

*No.* I wasn't having it.

I flapped my tail and swam up to him so my nose was level with his.

"Your birthday gift, my king," I said with scorn, "The gift your wife tasked Nerio to find is what caused his death. You might try to play that down, but it is the truth, and there's no denying it." I leaned in so close that he might feel the intense pain wafting off my body. "This is Atheana's and your fault.

And I will never forgive you for it. Not until you know the pain I feel."

I practically spat the last words, and when he grabbed for me, I ducked and swam under his arm back to Nerio. My gaze drifted to his lifeless body.

"Now leave me to mourn the loss of my love. And don't speak to me again."

Atheana and Neptune stared at me for several seconds. My brother opened his mouth to speak again, but Atheana wisely grabbed his arm and shook her head. Keeping her hand on him, she swept low to retrieve the chalice, then led him to the rear of the main hall to the palace interior.

Only then did I release the bubbles of agitation I'd been holding inside as I cursed the chalice, hoping it choked them each time they drank from it. Then I turned my attention to my Nerio.

I ran my fingers through his blond hair, letting the wet locks curl around my fingers. His gold, nautilus shell necklace glinted in the pale light, and in a sudden burst of need, I untied the necklace from his neck and fastened it around my own.

I might have lost Nerio, but I would carry something of him with me for the rest of my life.

I didn't return to the palace after we put Nerio in the Marsili volcano to return his body to the bottom of the sea from whence he came. Sebastian and the other fishes tried to console me, but I brushed them away. There was no consoling me. My niece Ginevra approached and tried to hug my tail, and after giving her a moment, I smiled weakly at her and pushed her gently back to her mother. While I may despise her mother, the little mermaid had done nothing to me. I wouldn't take my anger out on her.

That I would save for her mother.

Her horrible mother and father.

I couldn't bring myself to look at Atheana. Or at Neptune.

They robbed me of joy and happiness, of love and a future. My life was nothing but empty shadows because of them. And they did not seem to care very much.

And the idea of returning to the bright color of the palace sickened me. I swallowed back burning acid as I swam away. I went to the only place I felt matched my emotions.

My lair.

The dim interior and swirling cauldron were what I needed. It was my solace, my refuge, the one place where I didn't share any memories with Nerio, the one place that was mine and mine alone.

The seashell amulet rested lightly against my chest, and it was like I could feel Nerio with me through its comfortable weight.

I ran my fingers through my hair.

Now that I was alone, what was I going to do?

Sitting on the edge of my cauldron, I flapped my deep blue-purple fins and considered my options.

For the first time in my life, I didn't know what to do. Separated from Neptune and the palace and his subjects, it was just me.

I didn't feel like I fit in anywhere. How could I when everything merman and mermaid reminded me of Nerio? Of his eyes like a churning river and his hair as bright as the sunlight that penetrated the surface of the sea. Of his teasing smile and brave nature and kind hands.

Oh, my aching chest!

My flukes fluttered as I thought of him. My scales shimmered in the pale light of the cauldron, the blue even brightening as they shone.

*Blue*.

The same vibrant blue as Neptune's tail.

Hot rage burned through me. I hated anything that might tie me to the sea king!

Even my own tail.

I panted through my gills as I stared at my tail, the furling flukes and the glittery scales, and I made a decision.

I didn't *have* to be a mermaid anymore. At least, not one that matched Neptune. I could sever myself from him for good and make my body my own.

Turning to the cauldron, I peered into the bubbly surface. My reflection wasn't one of Neptune, thankfully. My hair was more silvery and longer, my eyes were icy gray, not bright blue, and I didn't have a huge beard covering my face.

But my tail. I curved it up until it was behind me, and I could see its reflection in the bubble.

And the fact I was a mermaid. If I was a mermaid, I was under Neptune's control – I was a subject of Atlantica. But if I changed the mermaid tail and never returned . . . well, that just cut Neptune from me even more.

I flicked my fingertips over my cauldron until the bubble shifted, showing the shining palace. It was as if nothing here had changed, as if the best merman in the sea wasn't gone.

Yet, I realized that if I left the kingdom and to be on my own, maybe others would want to do the same.

A smile curled against my lips. Or might be encouraged to do so.

My eyes snapped back to my reflection.

First things first – time to get rid of this tail.

## Chapter Four

In front of me, I placed an array of strange and unusual sea-faring ingredients to help achieve my goal and rip myself from all things Neptune: twisted sea-tree roots, dried starfish, and bits of crushed seashell and sea urchin. With deft sweeps of my hands, I mixed them in my large, steaming cauldron and muttered ancient incantations under my breath. My confidence in my abilities grew the more I chanted. The water around me quivered in small waves as I moved.

I flicked my eyes open, revealing their piercing ice-gray that reflected in my cauldron. Peering into the swirling, bubbling mixture, I searched for signs of the magic to invoke my desires.

At first, the potion was stubborn and resisted my efforts. The mixture shifted from blue to green to a murky black. Blowing out a bubble of frustration, I grabbed a hollowed-out shell cup and dipped it into the potion.

I studied the potion in the cup, then raised the cup to my lips as my long silver hair cascaded down my back. The potion began to boil and hiss, and I closed my eyes and drank.

Nerio's nautilus amulet seemed to vibrate against my cool skin as the potion exploded in my throat, sending a blast of energy shooting throughout my body. I choked and grabbed my neck. My body was wracked with searing pain as the magic potion coursed through my veins.

Crying out, I dropped the cup as the magic surged against my skin, and a tearing and expanding sensation unfurled throughout me. I was afraid to open my eyes.

*What have I done?* That was my first thought, followed immediately by a second.

*Did it work?*

When I finally gathered my courage and looked down at myself, what I saw was both shocking and exhilarating. I hadn't just transformed my tail – my body was no longer that of a mermaid at all. My curves rounded out fuller than I had imagined they could, and my skin from the chest down was no longer brilliant blue scales but smooth and slightly slippery to the touch. And black, all the darkest black, ending in tentacles. *Tentacles*! Or more like arms with how I was able to use them. Six arm-like tentacles writhing around me instead of a tail.

As I flicked the tentacles up and around, I noted they weren't pure black. When I lifted the tentacles, trailing my pale hand along their marvelous lengths, I saw the suckers underneath were a vibrant violet – the most vivid purple I had ever seen in my undersea life. I don't think even the land-walkers had anything this beautiful in their human world.

I grinned as I studied my beautiful new form.

Nothing like Neptune. Nothing like a mermaid. I was now dark, focused, and, most importantly, my own person.

The next Neptune saw me, he'd know that our ties were severed. He might yet be my brother, but in name only. I was now a mighty squid compared to his weak merman form.

I touched my hair. What else had changed?

I raced to my mirrored vanity to check my reflection.

My hair, still full and wild, had turned mostly white with remaining streaks of silver at the sides. My mouth was wider, my lips fuller, and my arms more round instead of the thin, sickly arms of my mermaid form.

This new form was strong, powerful, and commanding. Powerful enough to take on the king of the sea?

Perhaps.

Then another thought struck me as I gazed at myself. Had this transformation changed my magic? This bodily change was by far the most daring spell I had worked in all my time as a sea-witch, and didn't I look more like a sea-witch in full now?

Yes, I did.

It had to follow that my magic changed, too. That I could do more, that my skill was greater and more potent. Enough to challenge the greatness of King Neptune?

Perhaps.

*It remained to be seen,* I thought as I flicked my long-fingered hand through my hair. But if honing my magic meant one day I might have my vengeance and even wrest control of the seas from the sea king and his pathetic wife, then I'd toil day and night to make that happen.

Taking a moment to look at my surroundings, I evaluated my new existence. I couldn't live at the palace ever, not after this, not anymore, not with this body and every corner filled with memories and reminders of Nerio.

Instead, I decided to head to the palace, gather the rest of my belongings, and leave that part of my life behind forever.

I had Nerio's nautilus amulet that rested ever close to my heart. That was all I really needed from my former life.

It was time for Nerissa, the sea-witch, to start her new life.

Late that night, once any surface light had ebbed and the castle was bathed in shadows, I returned to the palace. Neptune was probably tucked into his kelp bed with Atheana, his children asleep in their nursery. All tucked in and safe while my Nerio slept the eternal sleep in the bowels of the seabed. Anger flared inside my chest like the sunlight on the water's surface as I crept into the main hall.

I had to get used to using my new body, which was not quite as sleek as my previous mermaid form but much more useful. My tentacles were like extra arms that could move and bend and grab.

*Much* more useful.

The swordfish guards' eyes widened when they saw me, but with a tiny bow of their heads, they let me pass.

They had to. I was still the king's sister, after all. And technically, the palace was still my home.

*Not for much longer.*

Whipping my tentacles under my hips, I rose to my chambers, and grabbing a large bag, I placed my most beloved and necessary items inside. Truthfully, I probably hadn't needed so large a bag. Few items remained in my room that I needed or wanted. I took a moment to float in the middle of my royal chambers and look around at the remnants of my past life one last time and realize how little of it mattered.

None of it mattered now. Not with Nerio gone. These items, these chambers belonged to someone who no longer existed. With a heavy, bubbly sigh, I closed the bag and exited the room.

And ran smack into Neptune who floated in the hallway outside my door.

"Neptune!" I shouted in a raspy voice. Ohh, my voice had changed a bit, too.

His face bore evidence of his sorrow that did not sway my steeled heart. He might be saddened over the loss of Nerio, but I had lost myself when I lost him. Neptune was still Neptune, while I had to become someone different, someone new. Someone who didn't have Nerio.

I despised his mockery of sorrow as much as I despised his and Atheana's role in Nerio's death.

"What are you doing, Nerissa? Where have you been?" His watery blue eyes roved over my body. "And what has happened to you? To your tail?"

I lifted my chin at him. "I'm no longer a mermaid. As such, I am no longer a subject to you or Atlantica. I'm leaving. I'll stay outside Atlantica in my cave."

He leveled his gaze at me. "You don't have to do that. This is always your home, no matter how you look."

"Really?" I asked with a smirk. "Because you treat those who aren't merpeople with the same respect as those with beautiful tails?"

"Nerissa –"

I could hear in his voice that I had hit a sore spot. Neptune had always given preferential treatment to the merpeople over the other fish in his kingdom. It was a character flaw that he tried to hide, but I had seen it more than once. My cheek twitched as my smirk deepened on my face.

"I have made my decision. Now move out of my way. Or I will move you." I raised a curled tentacle to show him I meant business.

I honestly expected him to put up more of a fight, but the weakling king bowed to my commands and swam to the side.

That was all it took. Lifting my bag over my shoulder, I shoved off with my tentacles and swam out of the palace.

Hopefully, for the last time.

# Chapter Five

The next few days passed in a blur, between me battling my mourning over Nerio and coming to terms with my new existence outside Atlantica. At first, all I did was lie in my sea-shell bed that I had padded with kelp, listening for the noises that were common in the palace but not here. Only the quiet lapping of water against the cave walls and the gentle skeleton bones rattle lulled me to sleep at night, and it was not enough.

Most nights, I stared at the dark water, thinking about Nerio and a future that never was.

And my hatred for Neptune and his kingdom grew as a lead ball in my belly. One that I fed with anger and sorrow and vengeance.

It was a lonely existence.

But it gave me plenty of time to think.

I have to admit, however, my first attempts at revenge were juvenile at best. With my confidence in my magic skills growing, I decided to try my hand at driving a wedge between Neptune and Atheana, at making them feel the raw despair of losing a loved one.

Something to lure Neptune away from Atheana – another mermaid, perhaps?

It seemed at once too much and not enough, but this was my first try, after all. And if it worked and he fell for the mermaid I created especially for him, then perhaps some of my unending ache might not eat away at my insides so much, like the little fishes ate at the seaweed until it was nothing but a bare stalk.

That was me – the bare stalk.

Creating a mermaid was something unique and unfamiliar to me – I had created waves and thunderstorms and seagrass and kelp forests to trap sinking sailors and fishermen, but an entire mermaid? And each time I used my magic, the storm seemed to leave me or the sea-worn and ragged.

It made me wonder if there was something changed in my magic. A price that had to be paid for its execution.

That, however, was a thought for another day. Right now, my concern was how to craft a mermaid out of magic.

Studying my cauldron, it spoke to me. I gathered fish bones, squid ink and cuttlefish venom, tuna scales, Neptune grass, and red coral. Crushing the coral, grass, and bones together, I poured them into my cauldron that bubbled and shimmered. With an ancient chant, I drizzled in the ink and venom, and then I laid the scales out in the form of a mermaid.

I waved my hand over the concoction, ready for a finely formed mermaid to emerge from my mystical bubble, when a sudden pain exploded in my chest, as if someone had struck me with a hammer.

Something dark and sinister whispered in my ear. "Your magic is a curse," the voice spoke inside my head, spiking like a headache. "There's a price to pay."

I recoiled in horror, realizing the truth of the words echoing in my head. My magic had always been robust, but now there were consequences in using it. As the most significant magical attempt in my life, the cost now was obvious. Had there always been some cost of which I hadn't known before? Some sacrifice? That prospect sent a shudder down my spine.

*Nerio.*

I shoved that thought from my mind. I wasn't going to assume the blame for his death. His life was too great a cost for the minor spells I had cast in the past. It wasn't my fault he had died.

This time, evidently, I hadn't paid the right price, or the shock to my chest was not enough of a price to pay, because the form flatting above the bubble turned blue-gray and split into two.

No mermaid – instead twin eels emerged from the mess, from the flotsam and jetsam of my mixture. There was scree and bream everywhere.

What was I going to do with two eels?

They blinked their big eyes at me, appearing as shocked to be here as I was to see them.

I moved to brush them away when one of them slid against my arm, its eyes closing slightly.

Was it ... was it nuzzling me?

Its twin joined him, curling around my other arm and peeking at me with wide, blinking eyes.

Oh, the poor things. In truth, they were nothing more than babies, created out of nothing and with no one to protect them or show them the ways of the sea.

At that moment, I decided I'd take them in. I was lonely anyway, and the devout way these eels looked at me made my heart surge in a manner it hadn't since Nerio –

I shook my head. No, I wouldn't think about him now. It would taint this moment with my new baby pets.

I tickled a finger under each of their chins, and they cuddled against me more, closing their big eyes.

"My babies," I whispered to them.

Adopting them was a sound idea, and a slender smile tugged on my tight lips. It was the first time in a long time. Though the spell had failed, I appreciated these little eels and made a space for them in my cave and in my heart.

"What are you called?"

They made matching hiss-like sounds, nothing that sounded like a name.

I glanced at the mess remaining from the attempt to create a mermaid – bits of bone and ink tainted the bubble rising above my cauldron and floated in the water. I thought of the words I used to describe the mess, scree and bream.

Those sounded like perfect names for these babies created out of a mess I'd made. I tickled their chins again as they curled around me.

"Scree and Bream," I said as I looked lovingly from one to the other, my failed plot to ruin Neptune momentarily forgotten. "Do you like those names?"

With my eels silently curled around me, I felt less lonely. Maybe that was the key. Maybe I didn't need Neptune and the palace, but I needed something, some merpeople, or some activity outside of myself to help me occupy my time.

That was something to consider later. For now, Scree and Bream were a great start.

My new friends kept me company as I adjusted to my new living situation. While I was at first worried I'd be bored and lonely, I was not. needed caretaking, and they frolicked in the waves with me when storms raged on the surface – storms I created so we might have fun in the waves. We chased fish and collected items from the seabed to refill my magic jars.

It wasn't the joy I had with Nerio, but it brought some measure of happiness to my dreary life.

I had tried to conjure more magic that might increase my power against Neptune, yet even when my magic was successful, nothing seemed quite right.

Until one morning, as I applied sea-hare ink on my wide lips and admired my appearance in the mirror, my babies careened into my lair, sleek and quiet.

"Ursula, you have a visitor," Bream hissed.

Sometimes, the way they said *Ursula* reminded me of the way my name rolled off Nerio's tongue, and I had to push that heavy memory from my mind. Shove it hard away, as I often did when the memory of my lost love invaded this new life I had created.

I cleared my throat. "A visitor?"

Screen and Bream spun and swam for the lair's entrance. Sweeping my tentacles under myself, I followed, my curiosity piqued.

Very few visited me in my grotto. No merpeople other than Neptune. I had heard from a passing-by tuna that my nieces had clamored to visit but that Atheana had put a sharp end to those requests.

Maybe one day, one of my nieces would have their own mind and make their way to my lair.

Today was not that day. Instead, a young merman eyed the opening, his furrowed brow showing his hesitancy over the skeleton-surrounded cave that his blustering chest did not hide. In truth, he had nothing to fear. I didn't bite.

Unless, he wasn't here because he was lost or on some misguided dare. I wouldn't put such a thing past senseless young mermen.

I floated at the far end of the opening, studying him. He had black hair and a bright, iridescent yellow fluke – truly a beautiful color and not a color that I had seen before, like sunlight under the waves.

"Don't lurk in entryways, dear boy. Some might consider it rude," I called out from the cave's shadows.

His eyebrows flew high on his forehead.

"Are you . . . are you the sea witch?" he asked in a shaky voice.

I pulled back my shoulders. What was wrong with the lad?

"Who else would be here?" My voice was a bit sharper than I intended, but why was he here? What did he want? Then a thought occurred to me, and I narrowed my eyes. "Did Neptune send you?"

The merman jerked backward. "The sea king? No, why would he send me?"

*Good question.* I waved him in.

"Come in and tell me why you're here."

He looked around the cave entrance, and then as if he was afraid the skeleton might come to life and eat him alive, he ducked low and quickly swam into the cave.

I led him to the open area of my lair where my cauldron bubbled lightly near the center. His eyes were rounder than dried sand flowers as he gawked at my home.

*How rude.*

I twirled around him in the water, letting one of my tentacles trail along his shoulders. Scree and Bream swam to my side, their silvery eyes riveted on our visitor.

"I don't have many visitors. Come, tell me why you are visiting the sea witch."

With a final frantic glance around the lair, his gaze landed on my cauldron.

"Is it true you can do magic? I've heard that the most recent storm that destroyed the pirate ship was your doing."

His voice strengthened as he spoke, as if he was in awe of such a thing. I couldn't help letting a sly grin curl my lips.

"Yes. Why? Are you here to complain about the destruction?"

The boat had sunk not far from Atlantica, and there it would reset at the bottom of the sea until a brave soul decided to investigate the human junk it contained. Useless junk, most likely. Who needed that land-walker garbage?

The merman shook his dark head. "No, actually, I came to ask if you use it for things other than storms."

My smile slipped, and I rested a long finger against my cheek. What was this merman up to? Did he have a sea slug under his scales?

I wiggled my fingers toward him, my red-tipped nails crimson blurs in the water. "A little magic, you could say."

He averted his gaze, suddenly finding the stone floor of my cavern very interesting. "Do you think, I mean, can you . . ." he sputtered.

"Spit it out, merman. What do you want from the sea witch?"

"A chance for Ledea," he blurted.

I had slid my gaze to my fingertips, only to snap my head up.

"What's a Ledea?"

His face twitched. Had I offended him?

"Not what. Who. Ledea. She's Saagar's daughter. He intends to marry her to Okeanos, but I don't think she wants that. At least, that's what she told me."

Saagar – a close confidant of Neptune's. *Interesting*.

"And what? You want her to marry *you* instead?"

He nodded, a smile cresting his face for the first time. "Yes! But I fear she might see me only as a friend. So if you could charm me or something . . ."

"To make her fall in love with you?" One of my silver eyebrows rose on my broad forehead. This poor lad had no idea of how magic, real sea magic, worked. "That's not quite a boat in my cove, but maybe I can help."

His dark eyes glittered as his entire face brightened. "You can? You will?"

I swirled my tentacles down to my cauldron and rested on elbows on it, leaning over the steamy, bubbly top.

"Well, yes, but not for *free*. There's no such thing as a free meal, my merman."

His entire body stilled and his shoulders slumped.

"Not for free?" he said quietly.

*Really*. Where did merpeople get the idea that magic came without a cost?

There was always a cost.

Sometimes too large a cost.

Maybe it was time for Neptune's subjects to learn this. For Neptune to learn this. He and Atheana had abused my magic for free for too long. And I had paid the ultimate price.

"No, but we can work out some terms." I rested my chin in my hands and my gaze on him as he considered. The floor interested him again.

"I don't have coin or anything. What do you want?"

I did not fully hear him – not because he was speaking quietly, but because my mind was working. Conjuring. Conspiring.

A burst of inspiration hit me at how I might carve away Neptune's kingdom. It was not anything massive or immediate or shocking, but something that would tear the threads of his kingdom away one by one.

I lifted myself and swam for my cabinet of potions and ingredients. I might hate the humans, but their jars were useful. Maybe I'd head out to the sunken ship later and see what I might find.

Right now, though, I had a merman to fry. I set the jars by the cauldron.

"It's pricey, and there's a time limit, if you will. I can't keep my magic going indefinitely after all."

His entire face twisted with confusion. I gave him a patronizing smile.

"What I mean is, I can help you, a bit. I can't guarantee she'll fall in love with you, but I can help *you* make that happen. You have four days to have her agree to marry you. I'll give you a charming personality, rich black hair, a slick tongue with the right words, everything you need to make any mermaid think you're a catch."

He rubbed his hands together. He was almost there but might back out if he heard the terms.

"If I'm everything she wants, then that should be easy," he admitted eagerly.

"Great!" I flipped my hand over the cauldron, and a golden scroll appeared that listed all the terms.

"What's that?" he asked.

I took a deep breath and leaned over the black cauldron again, shoving the scroll at him.

"The terms. If you get her to agree to marry you in four days, then this agreement disintegrates in my cauldron. If not, then the mermaid goes her own way, and you belong to me."

He had been reaching for the scroll, and his hand abruptly stopped. "What does that mean? Belong to you?"

I licked my full lips, biding my time because I didn't know yet. An assistant? A spy? A decoration for my wall? That was a problem I'd deal with later.

"I will own you and you'll become part of my lair." It was a pat, vague answer, but it was what I had. Time to see if it satisfied this desperate merman.

There was a long pause before he reached for the scroll. I bit back a smile – of course he reached for it. Desire was a powerful motive.

Just look at what Atheana had achieved with my fish-belly brother.

I handed him a bone quill tipped with octopus ink to sign, but as he reached for it, something else occurred to me. If he did get the girl, then I would be left empty-handed. I snatched the scroll back.

"There's one more thing. These are merely the terms of the contract. You still need to pay the magic cost. To conjure it."

"Wait, the cost? I thought –"

"Contract terms are different than costs, my dear," I said with a tight smile. "After all, if you get the mermaid, what payment do I have?"

"What do you want?" He still held the quill in his hand. I hadn't lost him yet.

My smile widened. "Your scales."

He looked down at himself, his bright yellow fluke twitching. "My – my scales?"

I snorted at his hesitancy. "Please. I'm giving you the charm and hair and words to make her choose you. If she can't love you because of your tail, do you want to marry her?"

My sound logic must have struck a chord because he shook his head wildly. With renewed force, he snatched the scroll and signed.

*Oh, Poseidon!* How easy was that? What I'd do with him when he failed, that I'd have to figure out later. For now, the deal was done.

As he watched, I threw several of my ingredients into my cauldron, chanting in the ancient sea tongue, and the center bubble grew until it consumed the merman. His mouth popped open as he was sucked in, given a sparkle of charm and rich black hair, before his scales were ripped away, replaced by a plain, flat orange tail. I gathered the scales in a pouch, taking a moment to admire their golden shimmering before tucking the bag in my cabinet.

Then I tapped the top of the bubble, and it burst in a bloom of gaseous steam.

The merman, his skin shining over a bland tail, surged upward.

As if a shark was chasing him, he raced for the cave's opening.

"Four days!" I shouted as the wake of his tail bounced against my body. "By sunset on day four! Then I'll come for you!"

The merman was gone. Scree and Bream had hidden in the recesses of the cave while I had worked. I grinned at them.

"Ready to help Momma?" I asked. They undulated in the waving water. "Follow him, and make sure she does *not* say yes."

Cheating? Maybe. My eyes fell on the withering polyps near the entrance of the cave. But I'd do what I must to bring that prideful Neptune, and his kingdom, under my control.

The eels took off after the merman, ready to do my bidding.

What good, loyal babies I had.

The curse of my magic held tight to the poor lad, and he learned a harsh lesson about the nature of love. The heart wants what the heart wants, and Leada didn't want him. She rejected the hopeful young merman outright and was betrothed now Okeanos.

The poor lad completely misread the situation, and now he was mine. I had watched his humbling, sometimes embarrassing efforts to woo Leada with my cauldron for four long days, and when the sun set on day four, I raced from my lair after him.

The polyps in my cave had given me the idea. Why not make my own subjects in my own shadowy kingdom? If one merperson came to me, others certainly would follow, and one by one, I'd collect those sad souls in my lair.

And this soul would be my first. My experiment. And oh, Poseidon! I hoped my coy plan worked.

He was swimming away from Leada's home, his head low and that sparkling charm dimmed. The spell was wearing off.

He evidently did not see me until I was right upon him.

"So it didn't work. Poor merboy. You should learn, even the best of magic rarely works the way you want."

His head popped up and he opened his mouth to speak, but I pointed my finger at him. An electric-like glow snapped at his body, encasing him until he withered away to a sad, gray-green polyp. I snatched him around his thin neck and dragged his tiny body to my cave. I plopped him at the front of the cave entrance where his tiny tendril legs gripped to the stone, attaching to it, and there he would spend the rest of his miserable life.

My first, tiny subject.

And how easy it was. Almost too easy.

Scree and Bream swam up to me as I threw my head back and laughed hard enough to cause ripples in the water.

## Chapter Six

Over the next year, more and more merpeople came to me, making their requests, agreeing to my terms, and giving me payment. Some came prepared, had something of value for the price, and met the terms. They managed to avoid the curse of my magic.

Lucky them.

But those mermen and mermaids were few and far between.

Oh, how my grotto grew – decorated with plants and shiny items – treasures both human and sea. And my subjects grew as well, populating the entrance to my lair like a gray-green carpet, sweeping along in my wake every time I entered and exited like my subjects bowing before me.

I kept waiting for Neptune to shove his way into my space and demand to know what I was doing, but he was too busy to notice.

Of course he was. Though Neptune was king, he didn't truly care about his kingdom or those in it.

His fifth daughter had been born, a red-headed girl that was the split image of her mother. Of course, she was his favorite. The baby, the one that looked exactly like Atheana, and they gave her another oceanic-name. Pearl? Coral?

No, Marina. That's what my mirrored cauldron showed me. They even had a cake frosted with lotus flowers and water chestnuts.

Neptune had sent Tiberian with an invitation. Did that merman really believe I'd ever enter the palace again?

Not on his best day.

I did send a gift. It was a dried sand flower.

I thought it represented the delicate balance of the sea.

My polyp collection grew, but for some reason, I didn't feel the joy in my revenge. With the birth of the final merbaby and Neptune's and Atheana's celebrations, they broadcasted their joy from the dolphins to crustaceans to the littlest fish, not noticing anything outside of their happy Eldoris bubble. Though I should have felt empowered with my polyp garden of subjects, that I was getting my vengeance as my polyp garden grew, I didn't.

Something was missing.

As I rested in my lair with Screem and Bream lying next to me, I had a moment of softness. Maybe I wasn't feeling my revenge over all my loss for a reason. Maybe it was a sign I should reach out, try to rejoin the palace, try to make my peace and share in the joy that Neptune and Atheana seemed to find with ease. That their joy could become my joy.

Because I was not finding such joy. Not in my collection of merpeople polyps – my subjects – not with my magic, not with Scree and Bream, not alone in my lair.

I was lonely.

*That* was it. Everyone had someone.

Everyone except me.

I sighed and rolled over in my shell bed, letting my tentacles drape over the edge as I ran my hand through my white-silver hair.

No sounds, no waves, no evidence of anyone but me.

I had taken to watching the palace in my mirrored cauldron more and more, as if I might live vicariously through the magic of my bubbles that showed me the entirety of the sea.

I started to despise myself for it. *I'm better than this,* I lied to myself.

I knew it was a lie because I kept watching.

And I also wondered if rekindling my friendship with Atheana or getting to know my nieces might combat my loneliness.

Neptune, ugh. Maybe not him so much. But Atheana, Ginevra, and the rest . . .

It came as a surprise when Neptune showed up at the mouth of the cave one afternoon. Late-day shadows under the sea had already blocked the weak sunlight from my cave, yet he was resplendent in his shiny white beard, golden crown, and iridescent teal fluke, as if his most recent daughter, his family, his pride in it all, brightened him. I swirled my tentacles around me as I met him at the entrance. A sly smile slid over my lips when I noticed how he looked around uncomfortably at the gray-green polyps. Did he know that I was slowly stealing his subjects?

He couldn't have. Otherwise he never would have spoken the words that came next.

"Atheana is tired of your absence. She misses you and would like you to join us for a festival at the palace, meet your niece, and see your other nieces."

I crossed my arms over my bosom.

"What about you, Neptune? Do you want me to visit?"

He was quiet for several moments, but his piercing blue gaze remained steady. That impressed me. I had rather expected him to avert his eyes, maybe from embarrassment or shame. Instead, he held my gaze.

"Yes," he answered with a slight bow of his head. "The palace is your home and you should be welcome there."

I pursed my lips before I spoke. "It hasn't been my home for quite a while, but as a courtesy to your family, I will make a visit."

Not to him, but he didn't seem to hear the difference. The tightness in his face relaxed a bit. Maybe he really did want me to come to the palace.

"Wonderful. I'll let Atheana know. Tomorrow, then?"

I nodded, my hair swirling around my head. "Yes. Tomorrow.

Trepidation filled my chest like an inflated blowfish as I approached the brightly lit palace. Breathing deeply through my gills, I brushed my hair off my forehead and swam inside.

The main hall was draped in lotus and kelp and sea anemones in the most brilliant colors. Even I had to admit that Atheana and her servants had transformed the hall into something from an oceanic dream.

"Nerissa!" a voice called out.

I spun around just as dark-haired Ginevra slammed into my tentacles. How she had grown in the past year! Her delicate face turned up to me, her eyes wide and her mouth a perfect *O*. "You have tentacles. Are you an octopus now?"

My smile to her was kind. She hadn't done anything to me, after all. I cupped her cheek with my long, slender hand. "A squid, darling."

"Why? Don't you like your tail?"

I shook my head at her innocent and earnest questions. "Not as much as I like the tentacles. They are like arms. Look what I can do."

Then I reached up to the wall with one tentacle, plucked one of the lotus flowers, and gently tucked it behind her ear. She giggled tiny bubbles of laughter.

"Nerissa! You made it!" Atheana's voice carried through the hall.

I swallowed the lump that formed in my throat at the sound of her voice. Looking at her was going to be difficult, but I had come here in good faith, to try to reconnect with my family. I'd do my best with her.

I turned around to find Atheana's beautiful face and wide blue-green eyes. "Atheana. Thank you for the invitation."

I gave her the same credit I'd granted Neptune the day before. Her eyes never left mine – not once roving at my changed body or averting her eyes.

She lunged forward, as if to embrace me, then stopped short so as not to overstep. I was glad she hesitated. I didn't really want to touch her.

"The mermaids have missed you, and I want you to meet your youngest niece."

With a flap of her hand, she swam toward the sea king's table. Several merpeople swam about, eating and chatting and listening to music. Everyone seemed jubilant, and once I laid my eyes on the baby, I understood why.

She was a vision of mermaid perfection, with Neptune's eyes and everything else her mother. They did have a good reason to celebrate.

I leaned over the baby, who studied me with wide eyes and plump, grabbing hands. She had no fear of me. I reached a tentacle into the shell-crib and she gripped it with her tiny hand.

"A bold one, this baby," I commented.

Atheana and Neptune were was going to have her hands full with this daughter.

"Yes," Atheana said in a vague tone. She didn't get my meaning.

Neptune swam over and greeted me, more formally than he had when I lived at the palace. Yet he wore a smile on his face and showed me personally to my seat.

Other mermen and mermaids swam by and chatted with me, full of questions and kind thoughts. Many of them I hadn't seen since I'd left, and as much as I hated to admit it, I was enjoying myself.

Perhaps my instincts in visiting the palace and my family had been good ones.

Green turtles carried trays of snacks, and I loaded up a plate. Palace food had a certain appeal, and that was something I had missed. The mix of salty and savory was a fine treat for my tired palate, and I relished each bite as I listened to the music and watched the celebrants.

The water to my left coursed over me in a wave, and with a mouth full of seaweed, I turned my head to find the chair next to me occupied by a merman whose skin was tinged with green that contrasted with his sandy brown hair. His tail, a darker sea green, glinted in the light and was barely visible under the table.

Who was this merman? And why had he chosen to sit next to me?

"Hello," he said in a deep, rolling voice. His eyes squinted with a smile, narrowing enough to shadow the sparkling blue that rivaled the sea's surface on a sun filled day.

Why was this handsome merman speaking to me? I kept my face still and didn't answer.

"My name is Fontaine." He held out his hand, palm up, waiting for mine.

I blinked. An introduction? What was he doing?

Two could play his little game. I lifted a tentacle and placed the tip violet sucker side down in his hand.

He didn't even glance at it. Instead, he squeezed it gently. I slid my tentacle off his hand.

"You're Neptune's sister, Nerissa. I am so pleased to meet you."

I flipped my hair over my shoulder and leveled a hard glare at him.

"Why?"

His eyes widened slightly. Of course, they were more blue that I could have imagined. Bluer even than Neptune's, and the sea king would be furious to know that.

"What do you mean, why? I see a beautiful mermaid and I wanted to introduce myself."

With a grimace, I lifted several of my tentacles from under the table until their sleek black beauty was directly in front of his face.

"Mermaid?"

He shrugged. "You were a mermaid, until a short time ago, or at least I've heard. You're still half sea creature, so it doesn't matter to me."

An odd statement. "Why would it matter to you anyways?"

"Because I want to get to know you better. I've been waiting to meet you, but you've been absent from the palace. From Eldoris entirely."

It was then that I noticed his gaze shifted, moving briefly from me to the head table where Atheana sat next to Neptune, a condescending smile on her face as she watched this Fontaine fellow flap his tail next to me.

Then it hit me like a lightning bolt to my head.

The reason for the invitation, for the feast at the palace, for the kind smiles.

Atheana wanted me out of mourning. She and Neptune were tired of my existence outside of Eldoris and wanted me to meet a new merman and fall in love.

She was trying to replace Nerio.

My entire body tightened.

As if anyone could replace Nerio, replace him in my heart, in my life.

I started panting as my tentacles curled at my sides. My rage was a volcano of fury boiling the water around me.

*How dare they? How dare she?*

How dare Atheana think she could parade mermen around me as if I might pick a new heart, a new love, a new life, from her selection?

*How dare she?*

My jaw clenched so hard my neck ached.

"I'm afraid you have been sorely misled," I told him with a bite to my tone. "I'm not interested in getting to know anyone better. I'm only here to celebrate my niece. Then I'm leaving Eldoris."

And not coming back anytime soon, if at all.

"Oh, don't say that. Stay with me for a while."

He reached for my hand. That green mer-fool *reached for my hand.*

I snatched it back before his fingers could twine around mine and rose with a twirl of my tentacles. He was lucky I didn't turn him into a shrimp right where he sat.

"In fact, I'm leaving right now," I spat out.

His mouth dropped open, but only bubbles emerged. Thankfully he didn't try to follow me as I headed for the main hall door.

I had made my appearance, congratulated the happy couple, and now I could leave. I was done. This was the last straw. I no longer wanted anything to do with Atheana and her bubble of happiness. Her joy only angered me more.

I had nearly made it to the door when I heard a rush of water behind me. I spun to find Neptune swimming up.

"Nerissa! Where are you going? We have this fine feast and guests –"

"Guests?" I surged up and poke my finger through his long beard to his bare chest. "You mean that green merman who tried to woo me as if I was some blathering mermaid looking for love? What a fool you are, Neptune, to think so little of me."

He pulled his shoulders back and looked down his nose at me. "It was nothing like that. Atheana was just trying to –"

"I don't care what she was trying to do. No one and nothing will replace Nerio, Neptune. You should know that."

"You can't mourn forever, Nerissa."

His pretentious tone galled me, heating the fury that already burned in a hot ball inside me. Coming to the palace had been a huge mistake.

"I can mourn as long as I need. And as I am no longer a subject of yours, Neptune. I don't have to live by your dictates, nor do I need your permission to leave."

"Nerissa!" he shouted.

I swept up higher until my nose was level to his. "Do not speak to me that way. You think yourself a king, but you're no king to me. You and Atheana think you're so powerful that no one or nothing can touch you, but know this Neptune. After the loss of Nerio, I know that truth. One day you'll learn that truth, too, Neptune. And you'll learn that you're not as powerful as you believe yourself to be. King or not."

Before he could say another word, I whirled around and pushed off with my tentacles so my wake slapped his face.

I didn't look back.

He'd learn one day. Somehow, he'd learn there were limits to his power.

## Chapter Seven

I'll admit that I longed for a way to show Neptune what my curse to him the night of the celebration meant, but I lacked any idea of how to make that happen. What could I possibly do to show Neptune the limits of his power?

I spent weeks sulking in my lair, far from the palace. Some days I kept the thoughts of how to teach Neptune a lesson at the front of my head, a thought that drove my hand with potions and tethered my eyes to my cauldron. Yet day after day, I saw and produced nothing.

Other days, and I'll admit there were a few of those days, I missed the palace. I missed my old life – the friendship with Atheana, bonding with my nieces, dancing with Nerio, the kelp gardens – even my brilliant blue-purple tail. Going to the palace that night revived those more tender emotions in my chest. Those aspects of my old life clung like fish scales in my memory, dull on one side but shimmery on the other. And sometimes, those shimmery sides caught me unaware, attracted my attention, and tore at my heart.

How would my life be different if Nerio hadn't died? I'd still be a mermaid with a glistening tail. I'd still live at the castle, most likely married to Nerio. Would we have had a child? A mermaid with white-blonde hair and teal eyes, with a shining tail and bright smile – all the love that Nerio and I shared poured like salt water into a tiny being that was ours?

In moments like these, where my memories and imagination ran away from me, I laid on my bed with my tentacles dangling over the edge and left the emotional toll course over me in waves.

Those moments, however, were brief. On the heels of those imaginings was my fiery vengeance, kindled by anger and sorrow, over all I had been robbed from me.

One single moment, and a life that could have been was gone in a wisp of swirling sand below the waves.

And once my mind shifted and abandoned those memories, all I focused on was what I might do to reclaim what remained of my bleak future.

A keening came from the front of my lair, and I flicked my eyes in that direction. The polyps swayed in the rolling water that ebbed and flowed from the mouth of the skeleton. A slight smile tugged at my lips. My polyp garden continued to grow, my captive subjects beholden to me. That was a good start on my vengeance.

Then my cauldron bubbled. Something was going on – something with Neptune. I shoved myself up from my bed and swirled my tentacles behind me, propelling me toward my cauldron.

What was Neptune doing?

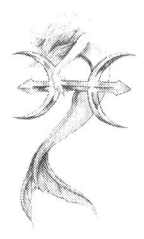

The surface of the black edge foamed up until one large bubble swelled above the rim of the cauldron and became my window to the crystal blue sea.

In the bubble, a stunning cove appeared – teal waters that lapped at a narrow sandy shore and foamed at the mouth of the undersea cave extending into the water. Large dark rocks surrounded the cove, creating a private sanctuary-like paradise. It was truly an impossibly beautiful place.

Neptune and Atheana lounged in that cove – Neptune in the water and Atheana sitting on a rock as water as blue as her eyes swirled around her and baby Marina splashed in the water right below her. A few other mermaids and mermen swam in the deeper water near the cave opening. My nieces swam to and from the narrow, rocky beach to their father and back in some sort of game.

Cute. Family time. With everyone.

Except me, of course.

I blew out a long, bubbling breath that pushed my swirling hair off my forehead.

Not that I'd want to be a part of that domestic bliss. So droll.

My cheek hitched with a hint of a smile.

Why not change that? End their fun little outing? A storm or large waves would be enough to disrupt their play.

I swept my long-fingered hand over the top of the bubble and mumbled a short chant. Clouds gathered directly above the water, creating a shift in the surf, and no more swimming games. I grinned to myself. That should be enough to drive them back under the sea.

Gray clouds amassed – not storm clouds but dark enough to obscure the cerulean sky – and the waves crashed. No longer gently lapping at the shore, the waves crashed with a vengeance.

My vengeance.

As I watched from my lair, Atheana glanced at the sky and Neptune flapped his tail to approach the shore, presumably to gather the children. The waves surged and something on the horizon caught my attention.

Is that – ? Is that a ship's prow?

Oh no. They were caught on the waves and heading right for the cove.

Sailors?

Or worse, fishermen?

I had to warm them. I had to help them get away, otherwise they'd be trapped by the oncoming ship. Neptune and Atheana might fend for themselves, but I didn't care about them. But my little nieces, they'd have no hope if they were trapped in the cove with fishermen.

If I could reach that underwater cave, I might be able to help the mermaids get away.

Grabbing a smaller bubble to keep watch on the cove, I thrust my tentacles behind me and wiggled my fingers in my wake so the water would push me faster.

Glancing at the bubble, I saw the ship sail into full view.

The sailors on deck were pointing at the cove and grabbing for hooked ropes and spears.

*Oh no!* I had wanted to teach Neptune a lesson and destroy his pride. Not his family. Not his daughters.

I might harbor anger toward my brother, but I wanted nothing to do with land-walkers. They were the ones who drove a hook through Nerio. They were more dangerous than Neptune might ever be.

These sailors, or whoever they were, meant business. I thrust my tentacles harder. The entry to the rear of the underwater cave was just ahead.

# Chapter Eight

By the time I surged upward to the mouth of the cave, Neptune was roaring about the humans as he shoved the mermaids and mermen under the deeper part of the sea opposite the ship.

Panic rose in my chest like a knife, slicing my insides as I scanned the water to see where everyone was.

My nieces were following Neptune toward the underwater cave – one, two, three, four, five – two were missing.

Baby Marina and Ginevra.

I searched the cove, looking for them in the churning water.

Ginevra had evidently swum toward her mother when the sailors arrived, most likely to help with the baby, but between the waves and the shouting sailors throwing hooks and spears at them, she was trapped. And Atheana, clutching a squalling

Marina to her chest, fought both the water and the land-walkers, working her way toward her eldest daughter.

I swept my hand over the water, hoping to calm the waves, but they had taken on a life of their own and were out of my control. Cursing to myself, I shoved out of the mouth of the cave toward her, one of my tentacles outstretched. If I could grab Ginevra, then Atheana and the baby could swim for safety at the mouth of the cave.

As I made it close to the ship, Atheana twisted and her panicked eyes found mine. She shoved Marina into my arms.

"Here, take her! I'll get Ginevra!"

Before I could say a word or convince her to leave, she was diving into the turbulent waves toward the dark head bobbing in the churning sea.

"Atheana!" I shouted, but my voice was lost in the crashing water, and then a sailor threw a spear at me. Shifting Marina in my grasp, I waved my hand at the sea again, and a wave knocked the deadly spear away.

With a final glance back at Atheana's bright red head breaking through the waves, I twisted my tentacles under my hips and raced to the cave. I dove under the surface, a squalling baby at my chest, and swam us both under the mouth of the cave.

Once underwater in the safety of the cave, I handed the baby to a frightened-looking mermaid who had gathered the rest of the children to swim them back to the palace. Neptune rose up next to me, his face dark with dread, a feeling that tore all the way to his heart, I'm certain. I was intimately familiar with that look, that feeling.

"Where's Atheana? Ginevra?"

I wiped my white hair out of my eyes. "Ginevra was trapped and Atheana went after her!"

I took off out of the cave before the rest of the sentence was out of my mouth, racing back toward the ship where Atheana dodged harpoons as she approached Ginevra.

Neptune followed, but I had a head start. Just as I reached the edge of the ship, trying to shove the vessel off-kilter with the force of my tentacles. Atheana had a hand on Ginevra's arm. She grabbed the mermaid at the same time as a barbed spear caught her in her upper chest. Atheana's eyes widened as all the color faded from her body. Even her bright hair faded.

I was dumbstruck, and my tentacles dropped from the hull.

"Atheana!" I shouted as I grasped Ginevra and yanked to my chest. Then I wrapped a tentacle around Atheana's waist and dragged her away from the ship.

Neptune met us at the cave opening as I was pulling the spear from Atheana's body.

My mind raced. Maybe I could say some words, a chant, a spell that might heal her wound. Maybe I could concoct a potion that might return life to her body.

But no. My once-friend, my nemesis, the mother of my nieces, was already the color of aged kelp, ready to become one with the ocean floor once more.

\*\*\*

Neptune roared as he swam up beside me and ripped Atheana from my tentacle. His bold face was stricken, nearly as pale as Atheana's, but the lines of his jaw and eyes were tight, as if he was holding back.

He *was* holding back. His rage and confusion and dark sorrow, he held all of that back so he didn't do something he might regret in front of his children.

"What have you done?" he rasped as he curled Atheana's limp form against his chest. "What have you done to my family? To *your* family?"

*Me? I didn't do anything!*

Yet, I had no words, nothing that might convey my own shock and horror at the events that had led up to this – the events starting so long ago with Nerio searching for a chalice for Neptune. How had it all gone so awry?

Other than the waves that I had commanded – those had been my fault – but then, if Neptune and Atheana had left as soon as the clouds gathered, maybe none of this would have happened.

If they hadn't been at that cove to begin with . . .

If there hadn't been a ship . . .

Too many ifs . . .

The water around me swished as the mermaid ushered Neptune's daughters, Ginevra and Marina included, farther away.

Smart mermaid, seeing the fury on Neptune's face.

"This is not my fault –"

His eyes narrowed. "Isn't it? You saw us in the cove and decided to dampen our day, bring clouds and waves, and on those waves came sailors and destruction."

I pressed my hand to my chest, my fingertips resting on Nerio's shell that yet hung from my neck. "I cannot be held responsible for the sailors –"

"Can't you though?" he roared, surging closer so his face, was close to mine, Atheana's body the only barrier between us. "If you hadn't brought the waves, the sailors would not have been swept off track and Ginevra would not have been trapped! You have betrayed me in the worst possible way! Betrayed your entire family!"

That did it. Hadn't he and Atheana betrayed me? He was the one who had brought his family to the surface to play! And if he blamed me for the actions of the sailors, then wasn't I in my right to blame him and Atheana for the loss of Nerio at those same hands? Hadn't I experienced the same loss, maybe worse because I had no reminder of Nerio while he had five, including his youngest who was the spit-image of Atheana? At least he had something.

What did I have?

*Nothing*.

And he was blaming *me*?

*Oh, no. Not today.*

I drew my shoulders back to face him straight on. "I didn't want this. But don't dare to speak of me of betrayal."

His eyes narrowed. "You bring destruction with everything you touch. With every flick of your fingertips. Stay away from us all. I know what you have been doing in your lair with your tainted magic and keeping my subjects as a way to punish me. No more. You are banished, and if I see you near my children or the palace or in Eldoris at all, I will take my trident and slay you myself."

Before I could respond, he turned his back on me, taking Atheana away to join her family who would bury her.

As I stared after him, insulted fury blaring through my body, I understood in that moment that I truly meant nothing to my brother. That he would continue to use all of his power of the sea against me. That my pain, my loss, all that was nothing to him. It was and always had been his kingdom, his family, and now his loss.

Before they exited the cave below the sea, Ginevra turned around and glanced over her shoulder at me, sorrow filling her wide eyes.

That was my last vision of my niece as the merpeople I had once called family abandoned me completely.

With a scowl painted on my lips, I waited until they departed the cave and I was left by myself again. Despised again. Shunned again. This time for trying to save the very woman who had robbed me of my love and my future – now I was banished for my valiant efforts.

Neptune knew nothing of betrayal, and though I had tried to help, tried to save them all the moment I saw that ship, he blamed me and dared to minimize my own trauma, my loss of my love. As if the loss of his love was greater, more painful than mine.

How dare he?

My fury burned hotter under my skin.

Did Neptune's selfish pride know no bounds?

My hands clenched hard against my tentacles. Evidently not.

Trying to quell my blazing rage and, truthfully, my indignation, I slowly swam back to my dark lair. My mind spun, trying to make sense of Neptune's words, my own emotions, my banishment, and the fact that Atheana had died. She, the woman who I blamed for Nerio's death was gone. And if I let Neptune's words influence me, she was dead by my hand. Indirectly by my hand.

I had my revenge then, didn't I?

At first I believed that losing Atheana would be enough to satisfy by vengeance against both her and Neptune. Now he knew the depths of my pain and we were even, but I didn't feel that way. The sea hadn't returned to balance. He blamed me for her death and banished me from Eldoris. Yet he still had adorable daughters to indulge in, to love him, to cater to him as Atheana had.

He wasn't any worse off, not really.

Not like me. I still had nothing but my lair, my eels, and my polyps.

I was merely the detested sea witch whom he looked upon with disgust. His own sister, and he couldn't bear to have me in Eldoris.

I couldn't imagine what horror stories he would tell his daughters about me. Others in the palace – his swordfish guards or his crab adviser – would hear those false rumors and make me into more of a villain that I already was.

I panted through my gills.

That was too much.

All of this had happened because of Atheana and her command to Nerio. Not because of me.

I narrowed my eyes at the waves bouncing against the walls of my lair.

He wanted to destroy me, and he could well make that happen.

*No!* I shouted in my head.

At that moment, I made up my mind, not just to have vengeance, but to destroy him and his entire family as he and Atheana had destroyed mine. Before he destroyed me. To take away everything from him, including his kingship, his precious Eldoris.

To make myself Queen of the sea.

To rob him of all his joy and make him one of the polyps in my grotto.

One day I would make all that happen.

*One day.*

*THE END*

# Read More!

**Want a bonus ebook** from the Glen Highland Romance and several other free ebooks? Love romance books, announcements, and discounts? Click the link or the image below to join my newsletter and receive *The Heartbreak of the Glen*, the free Glen Highland Romance short ebook, in your inbox!
Click here: https://view.flodesk.com/pages/5f74c62a924e5bf828c9e0f3

# Excerpt from Before the Glass Slipper

*Love Fairy Tale Retellings? Give the Before... series a try! Keep reading to discover Before the Glass Slipper for the story of the Evil Stepmother!*

## Chapter One

"Mother, please. Don't make me do this," I begged.

Over and over, I had begged, pleaded, even tried bribing, but to no avail. I was going to have to wed the miserable Seigneur Dubois in a fortnight, and no recourse had made itself known. From the tight lines around my mother's eyes, she was tired of hearing my protests.

"Corinne, I'll not have you behaving like this. I'm finished with this conversation, and so is your father. You will marry Seigneur Andre Dubois and be grateful. So many girls your age would be ecstatic to wed as accomplished a man as Andre."

*Accomplished.* That was a code word for old. And wealthy. Those were the sole concerns my parents had for my future. Marrying for love? They'd scoffed at the idea and sent me to my room. Then they had accepted the old man's offer on my behalf.

I understood their concerns. Father had worked hard as a merchant, buying rugs, furs, and fabrics from the docks and selling them to upscale lords, *comptes*, and even a few dukes, but local wars and pirating had plagued the shores of La Rochelle to the bustling town of Poitiers, and fewer goods had become available. Father's financial well-being had started to fall down the path to ruin. Plus, to hear Father tell it, the King's taxes had made his finances worse. They needed a solution, something to keep them in their home for the rest of their lives.

So they were *selling* me. No matter what pretty packaging they tried to wrap the news in, that was the ugly truth.

"Mother," I tried once more. Mother angrily waggled a finger at me.

"I'm finished. Now, go to your chambers and have Elise finish helping you pack. The seamstress will be here this afternoon to complete your gown. And your bridegroom is generous and sent you a fine wedding gift. I'll show you when you try on your dress." Here, her face brightened, the first time I'd seen such a look in longer than I cared to think on. "It is the most refined gift. You'll love it."

She may have been trying to sweeten the pot, but I knew it was nothing more than additional bows on the horrible present I was set to unwrap. I shuddered; the idea of unwrapping anything with regards to my bridegroom made my gorge rise.

When I entered my room, Elise gave me a gentle, closed-mouth smile. She was the only one in the house who commiserated with my plight. A plain, silver-edged glass hung near my water table, and I looked away. Since the announcement of my impending nuptials, I had avoided seeing reflections of myself anywhere, because it was my dark, ethereal beauty that put me into this position to begin with.

*Start this villain backstory today! https://www.amazon.com/gp/product/B09B2RFJN5*

# Excerpt from Before the Cursed Beast

*Love Fairy Tale Retellings? Give the Before... series a try! Keep reading to discover Before the Cursed Beast and download the entire book!*

## Chapter One

I rushed into the magician's study, my skirts whipping at my legs, my arms full of clay jars, and my heart full of fear.

It hadn't always been this way, with fear ruling my life. Years ago, when I was a girl, the magician had seemed like a guardian, a caring protector. He was my first love, my first kiss, my first role model. But once I started to learn magic and master it with skill, he had changed. No longer did I play with childish magic, training rodents as pets or opening flowers in a field. *Non*, real magic affected the hearts and minds of people, and Adolphe's behavior towards me changed as quickly as if I'd cast a spell on him.

When he used to speak to me with kind words, he now barked demands and insults. Where we had once worked side by side, he now banished me from the study and relegated me to demeaning cleaning and gathering chores. When once he had touched me with love and adoration, he now delivered his harsh words with a smack or a slap.

And I was disappearing.

Not really, not like magical disappearing where something is no longer present at all. *Non*, disappearing into myself, losing what I used to be, a cherubic girl who loved to play with her guardian and magic.

Now every aspect of magic frightened me, or worried me, as I waited for a curse or a heavy hand. I no longer smiled, and my once-shiny chestnut hair had become ashen, stringy. I had taken to sleeping in the kitchens, as I didn't want Adolphe to find me.

And it suited. I was treated as nothing more than a servant in what had once been my home. Why not sleep where the servants do?

"Salome! Where are you with my concoctions? Even a fool could work faster than you!"

Adolphe's harsh words exploded from his darkened study and carried into the hall where I juggled the jars. I held my breath as I walked, afraid of what he might do if I dropped a jar, or even almost dropped one . . .

I rushed into the study and placed the jars on his disheveled worktable. Gone were the days where I perched on the table and watched him work. Now I cowered behind it.

"Took you long enough," Adolph threw over his shoulder at me.

He faced his bookshelf, lifting the lids off glass jars and sniffing. Though his study was large, with vaulted ceilings reinforced with wood beams and a single long window at the far side of the room, Adolphe still took up so much space. He was tall, taller than most other men I'd met, limited though that might be, and his black velveteen cloak added to his dramatic flair. The olive undertone to his skin prevented him from appearing washed out, even in the dim light of the wall sconces.

"I had to find the right jars. There were so many in the cellar —"

"If you paid better attention, then maybe you'd find what you were looking for in a more timely manner." His tone grew more harsh as he spoke.

"I'm sorry, I —"

"I don't want to hear your paltry excuses," Adolphe bit back. "Now put the jars in the center of the table, with the earwig dust closest to me. Then leave and make yourself useful by cleaning the rooms in this tower. You've let it become filthy."

I bowed my head, trying to hide in the folds of my stained gray gown. When was the last time I'd worn a brightly hued gown, or one of rich jeweled tones? Or even a new one? Months? Years? This one lost all its color and barely reached my ankles.

"Yes, Adolphe," I answered, casting my eyes at the floor.

He grumbled to himself as I picked up the jars and moved them as he asked. I had grabbed the last one when it slipped from my shaking fingers onto the table. The jar didn't break, *thank the stars,* I thought in a panic, but the contents – powdered dung from the smell of it – spilled all over the table and his assorted papers and herbs.

My hands froze. Maybe I could clean it up before he saw. Maybe I –

Adolphe stopped his grumbling and whirled around. His black eyes blazed in his face, and I shrunk back from him.

"'Tis only the dung. I can clean it –"

Adolphe's hand slammed onto the table with such force, all the jars clinked on the table, threatening to fall over.

They didn't, and I released a slow, shaky breath. Then I looked up at Adolphe and cowered back more.

"Get you gone from here. You are as useless as a cane for a bird."

Grab the book here: https://www.amazon.com/dp/B09V9S6KR3

# About the Author

Michelle Deerwester-Dalrymple is a professor of writing and an author. She started reading when she was 3 years old, writing when she was 4, and published her first poem at age 16. She has written articles and essays on a variety of topics, including several texts on writing for middle and high school students. She has written over seventy books under a variety of pen names and is also slowly working on a novel inspired by actual events. Her Glen Highland romance series books have won *The Top Ten Academy Awards* for books, *Top 50 Indie Books for 2019*, and the *2021 N.N. Light Book Awards*. She lives in California with her family of seven.

Find Michelle on your favorite social media sites and sign up for her newsletter here: https://linktr.ee/mddalrympleauthor

# Also By Michelle

## As Michelle Deerwester-Dalrymple
## Glen Highland Romance

*The Courtship of the Glen – Prequel Short Novella*

*To Dance in the Glen – Book 1*

*The Lady of the Glen – Book 2*

*The Exile of the Glen – Book 3*

*The Jewel of the Glen – Book 4*

*The Seduction of the Glen – Book 5*

*The Warrior of the Glen – Book 6*

*An Echo in the Glen – Book 7*

*The Blackguard of the Glen – Book 8*

*The Christmas in the Glen — Book 9*

<u>The Celtic Highland Maidens</u>

*The Maiden of the Storm*

*The Maiden of the Grove*

*The Maiden of the Celts*

*The Roman of the North*

*The Maiden of the Stones*

*Maiden of the Wood*
*The Maiden of the Loch - coming soon*

<u>The *Before* Series</u>

Before the Glass Slipper

Before the Magic Mirror

Before the Cursed Beast

Before the Mermaid's Tale

## Glen Coe Highlanders

*Highland Burn* – Book 1

Highland Breath– Book 2
Highland Beauty — Book 3 coming soon

## Historical Fevered Series – short and steamy romance

*The Highlander's Scarred Heart*

*The Highlander's Legacy*

*The Highlander's Return*

*Her Knight's Second Chance*

*The Highlander's Vow*

*Her Knight's Christmas Gift*

*Her Outlaw Highlander*

*Outlaw Highlander Found*

*Outlaw Highlander Home*

## As M.D. Dalrymple - Men in Uniform

*Night Shift – Book 1*

*Day Shift – Book 2*

*Overtime – Book 3*

*Holiday Pay – Book 4*

*School Resource Officer – book 5*

*Undercover – book 6*

*Holdover – book 7*

<u>Campus Heat</u>

*Charming – Book 1*

*Tempting – Book 2*

*Infatuated -- Book 3*

*Craving – Book 4*

*Alluring – Book 5*

<u>*Men In Uniform: Marines*</u>

*Her Desirable Defender – Book 1*

Printed in Great Britain
by Amazon